Fields and flowers

Circle the unicorn below that matches this black shape.

Find 5 pink butterflies, then draw around them.

Draw over the dotted lines to finish the unicorns.

In the sky

Draw wings on the unicorns that don't have them.

Draw over these dotted lines to finish the rainbow. You can fill it in if you like.

How many birds can you count? Trace over the correct number.

4   5   6

Tiny friends

Connect the numbered dots in order, to finish the unicorn.

Draw wings on the two butterflies that need them.

Find 3 red spotted bugs, then draw around them.

1

2

3

4

5

6

7

8

9

Icy maze

Draw a line to show this unicorn the way along the icy path to her friend.

Draw around the narwhal above that does not match the others.

3 4

How many hares can you count? Trace over the correct number.

Enchanted forest

Find 1 squirrel, 2 owls and 3 rabbits, then draw around them.

Draw over the dotted lines to finish the moon.

How many unicorns can you count? Trace over the correct number.

4 5 6

Flower garden

Which unicorn will step over the most flowers? Follow the trails and count the flowers to see.

Find 6 bees, then draw around them.

Draw over the dotted lines to finish the flowers.

Night flight

Spot 3 differences between
these two dragons.

Find 5 bats, then
draw around them.

Draw more spots
on this unicorn.

Draw over the dotted lines
to finish the water creature.

Palace maze

Draw a line along the path to show the unicorn the way to the palace.

Draw around the flower above that does not match the others.

Draw over the dotted lines to finish the trees.

8

Tropical treetops

Connect the numbered dots in order, to finish the tree house.

Find 5 orange flowers, then draw around them.

How many parrots can you count? Trace over the correct number below.

5 6 7

Golden afternoons

Draw more leaves falling from the trees.

Find 5 squirrels, then draw around them.

Draw over the dotted lines to finish the toadstools.

Draw around the hedgehog above that does not match the others.

Under the waves

Are there more orange or pink fish?
Draw around the answer below.

Find 3 more unicorn
seahorses like this,
then draw around
them.

Draw over the dotted
lines to finish the
seaweed.

Crystal cave

Which unicorn will step over the most crystals? Follow the trails and count the crystals to see.

Find another firefly just like this one, then draw around it.

Make patterns on this unicorn.

At the palace

Connect the numbered dots in order, to finish the palace.

13

Spot 3 differences between these two unicorns.

Follow the trails to see which frog jumps into the pool.

Island tour

Draw a line to show the unicorn the paths to fly along to the island at the rainbow's end.

Spot 3 differences between these two castles.

Draw over the dotted lines to finish this whale.

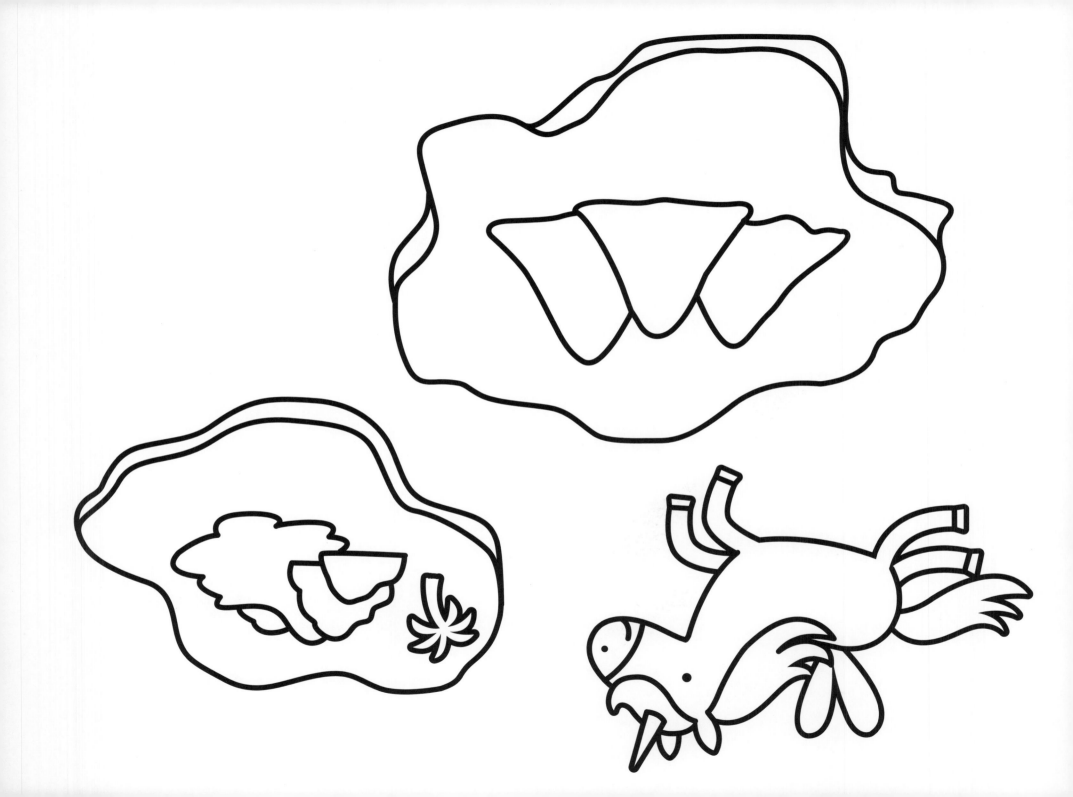

Snowy winter

Draw more mountains below.

Find 5 penguins, then draw around them.

Draw over the dotted lines to finish the patterns on the scarves and blankets.

By the waterfall

Draw splashes of water
around this purple unicorn.

Which frog will jump on the
most lily pads? Follow the trails
and count the lily pads to see.

Are there more red or
blue dragonflies? Draw
around the answer below.

Back to the stables

Draw a line to show the unicorn the way to the stables.

Draw around the rabbit above that does not match the others.

Find another unicorn that looks just like this one, then draw around it.

Starry nights

Draw over the dots to see what the sleeping unicorn is dreaming about.

Draw around the unicorn below that matches this black shape.

Draw over the dotted lines to finish the four stars.

Above the clouds

Follow the trails to see which unicorn took off from the palace.

Find 3 rainbows, then draw around them.

Draw over the dotted lines to finish the three clouds.

Competition time

Find 6 fairies, then draw around them.

Draw around the unicorn ...... that does not match the others.

Draw over the dotted lines below to finish the crown.

2nd

1st

Mighty mountains

Draw a line to show the unicorn the way to the top of the highest mountain.

Draw over the dotted lines to finish the trees.

Spot 3 differences between these two mountain goats.

Find 3 flying eagles, then draw around them.

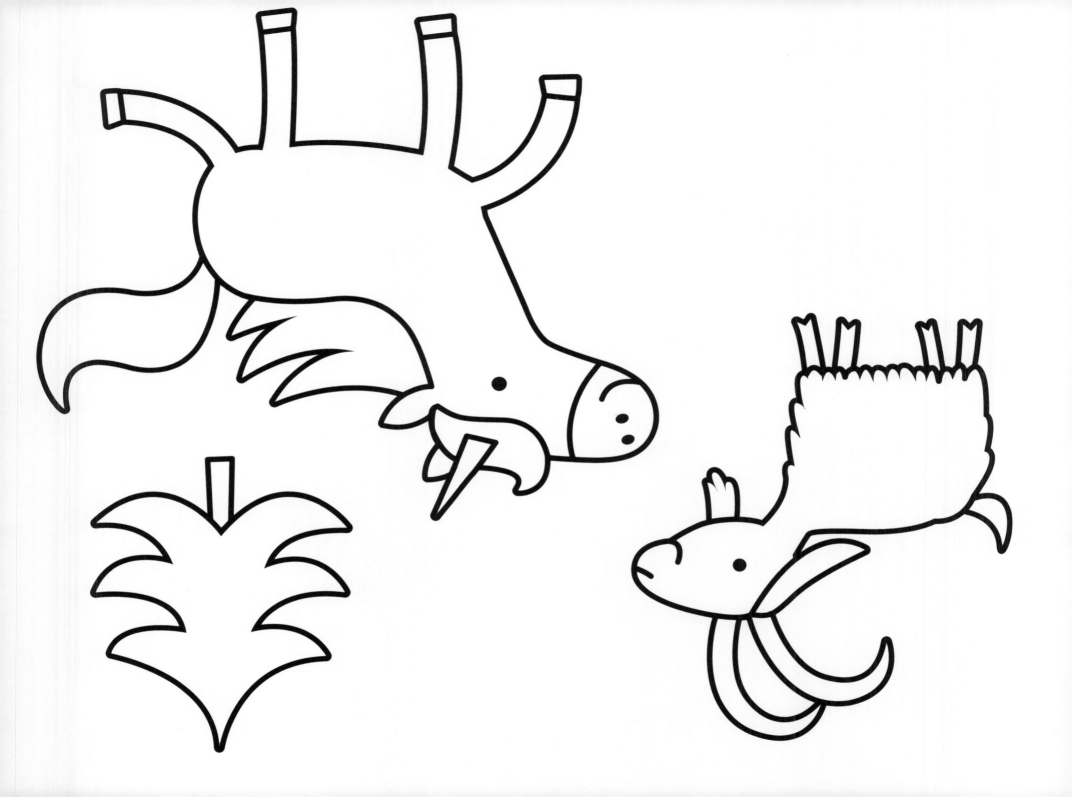

Sunny days

Draw a line between each pair of matching unicorns.

Draw over the dotted lines to finish the gate.

Count the spots on each unicorn, then trace over the numbers.

5

6

7

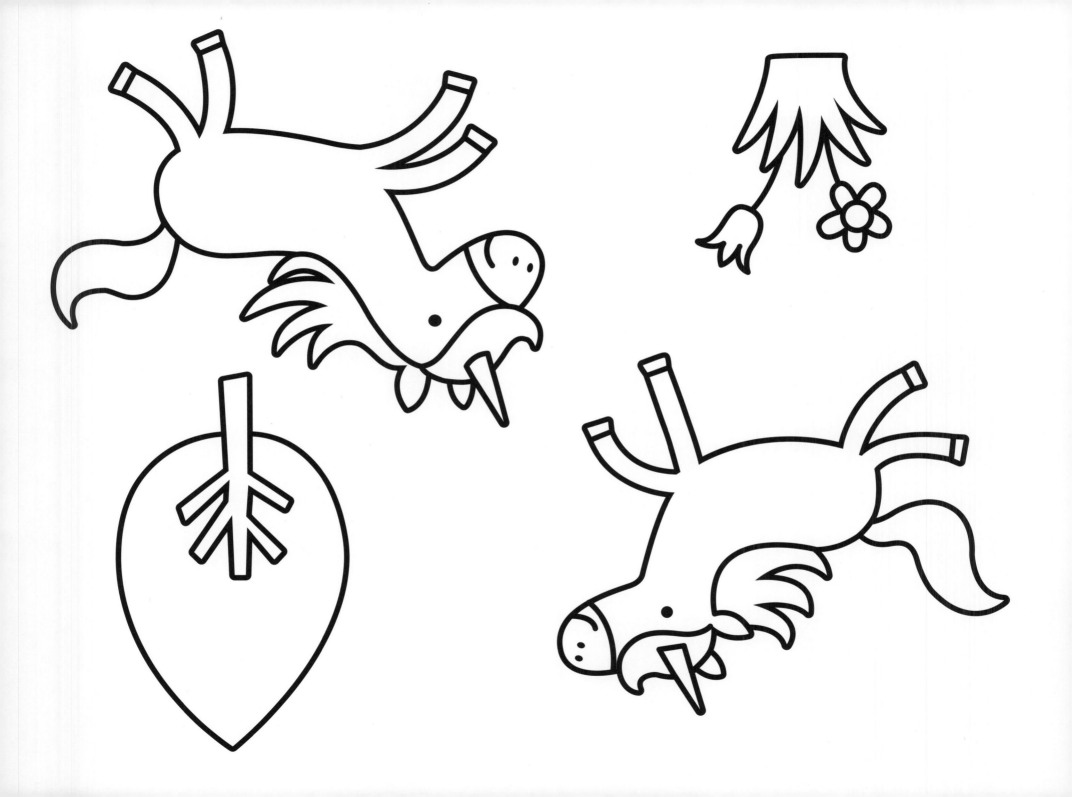

Party time

Draw over the dotted lines to finish the cake.

Draw a line from each cupcake below to the one that looks just like it.

How many mice can you count? Trace over the correct number.

4 5 6

Springtime

Draw a line from each baby unicorn to its mother.

Draw over the dotted lines to finish the fence.

Find 5 yellow flowers, then draw around them.

Follow the trails to see which rabbit will go into the burrow.

Christmas fun

Draw over the dotted lines
to finish the Christmas tree.

Find the star decoration
for the top of the tree,
then draw around it.

Spot 3 differences between
these two piles of presents.

Are there more red or green
decorations in the picture?
Draw around the answer above.

On the beach

Which unicorn will step over the most shells? Follow the trails and count the shells to see.

Draw over the dotted lines to finish the sun.

Draw a line between each starfish and the one that looks just like it.

Carriage ride

Connect the numbered dots in order, to finish the carriage.

4   5

3

6

2

7

1   8

Draw over the dotted lines to finish the wheels.

How many butterflies can you count? Trace over the correct number.

6 7 8

Spot 3 differences between these two unicorns.

Mermaid island

Follow the trails to see which one will lead to the mountains.

Draw over the dotted lines to finish the palace.

Find 1 snowman, 2 rainbows and 3 mermaids, then draw around them.

By the lake

Draw horns on the three unicorns that need them.

Draw over the dotted lines to finish the bandstand.

How many fish can you count? Trace over the correct number.

7 8 9

Moonlight magic

Are there more white
or golden stars? Draw
around the answer below.

Find 3 blue moths, then
draw around them.

Draw around the
sleeping unicorn
that does not
match the others.

Answers

You will find answers to all the puzzles on these two pages.

1 Fields and flowers

2 In the sky

3 Tiny friends

4 Icy maze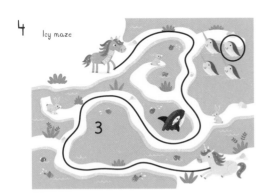

5 Enchanted forest

6 Flower garden

7 Night flight

8 Palace maze

9 Tropical treetops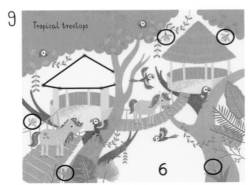

10 Golden afternoons

11 Under the waves

12 Crystal cave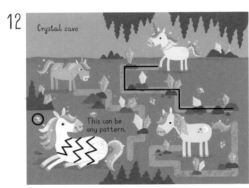

This can be any pattern.

13 At the palace

14 Island tour

15 Snowy winter

16 By the waterfall

17 Back to the stables

18 Starry nights

19 Above the clouds

20 Competition time

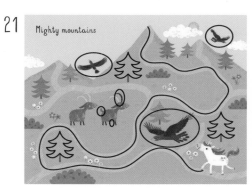

21 Mighty mountains

22 Sunny days

5   6   7

23 Party time

5

24 Springtime

25 Christmas fun

26 On the beach

27 Carriage ride

6

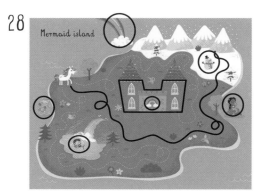

28 Mermaid island

29 By the lake

7

30 Moonlight magic